AN ODYSSEY

THE MAGIC BEGINS..

SHREE KRISHNA & DR. NEHARIKA SAXENA

I devote this book to my Father Dr. Hari mohan saxena,Late Mother Dr. Madhu Prabha saxena, sister Priyanka and grandmother Kamla saxena.

Contents

Foreword

This book is a magical odyssey into Shiva the absolute. This book explores him as a person and not as a diety. You will fall in love with him, reading this book, just like I did while writing. It is a journey of the faith, passion, romance, heartbreak, devotion, bravery and what not. This book gives faith to the hopeless and tears of joy to his devotees.This book is written in a simple yet charismatic style to lure the readers of all age. With lots of love to Shiva..the supreme. Enjoy the journey.

Preface

<u>THE GREAT BATTLE – AFGHANS AND THE LORD</u>

Set somewhere in the rocky terrains of Afghanistan, this is a story of a major battle that took place between the Anglo-Indian soldiers and the Pathans of Afghanistan.It is of the time when India was under the british rule.When the devout wife of the English captain did penace for Lord Shiv's blessings, the story took on a dangerous turn.It's a beautiful story of hope and faith, giving tears of devotion to anyone who reads it and instills in them faith in the divinity of Shiva, the supreme Lord.

<u>THE UNUSUAL CUSTOMER AND THE BLESSED CONCUBINE</u>

Now we come to a timeless tale... of beauty, passion and a compassionate heart. Of a demigod and his muse. A devotee and her lord. Set in a small village called Nandigrama , based on a prostitute called Mahananda, who was a great devotee of Lord Shiv. One day she gets an unusual customer(a merchant).The magic that ensues in their passion and the pious ending is worth reading. As the story unfolds the customer turns out to be lord Shiv himself in guise of a merchant.

<u>THE PRINCESS WHO BECAME A YOGINI...</u>

Her beautiful hair decorated with flowers, with a sweet smile on her face. Draped in a saree, still waiting for her soulmate, like a mermaid in the sea. This is a timeless tale of princess Kanya kumari and her battle of faith to win her beloved Shiva. It entails her fierce battle with a demon Banasura for whose destruction she incarnated.The marriage ceremony takes an omnious turn as the pangs of destiny wield up.

<u>EVERYONE HARPS THERE IS NO TIME</u>

The protagonist goes through the spur of the great Mount Kailash. This story is based on the holy Kedarnath yatra. The man undergoes grave difficulties on his yatra due to tripping of his pony. Its a story of a live encounter with Lord Shiv of a devotee.Its a perfect example of how his highness changed time dimension to help the poor man.

<u>I CAN FEEL YOU'RE HEART BEATS</u>

It is the story of a girl named Swati, who was suffering from schizophrenia, a mental disorder where you see hallucinations. She takes up devotion of Lord Shiv to reliev herself of the mental pressure. Lord kindly comes himself to help her in person to help her pass through this dreaded disease. They form a beautiful bond with each other. Although it ends up with her winning up from this disease, the love of lord resides in her heart forever, Inspiring her for the future.

<u>TO LAUKESH WITH LOVE</u>

It is the story of the innocent Saint Laukesh , a great mendicant who did penace to achieve salvation at lords feat. Many years had passed in his penace. Lord Shiv had meanwhile married Parvati. Laukesh couldn't handle the shock of his diety being a householder. Lord thus did a great penace for a thousand year to bring Laukesh back into the past time when Lord Shiv was unmarried. It's a story of his highnesses greatness and compassion to all those who seek his refuge.

<u>WHEN THE LORD READ FOR HIS DEVOTEE</u>

It's a beautiful story set in the state of Kerala, in a temple called Kottiyoor, the main deity was Lord Shiva. In the same place lived an ardent devotee of Krishna named Poonthaanam. His devotion transcended the boundaries of heart and soul. Thus Lord Shiva descended with his ghosts and wife to hear the bhagvatam preached by Poonthanam. Lets see what happened when the Lord read for his devotee.

Acknowledgements

Acknowledgements

I would like to thank God for giving me the power to believe in myself and pursue my dreams. I want to thank my parents, Prof. Dr. Hari Mohan Saxena and Late Dr. (Mrs.) Madhu Prabha Saxena. Thanks to both of you for your exceptional love and support. This thesis is nothing without your kind blessings. I dedicate this thesis with love to my Mummy and Papa, my sweet Lord Jagannathji and my revered grandmother Mrs. Kamla Saxena.

This book would not have been possible without the guidance and the help of several individuals who, in one way or another, contributed and extended their valuable assistance in the preparation and completion of this study. I take immense pleasure in expressing my sincere and deep sense of gratitude to my guide and mentor, Priyanka saxena (sister) for her encouragement and exemplary guidance throughout the course of my research. I couldn't have done it without a sister as friendly and understanding as you. It wasn't that easy to carry out research for this book without the flexibility and freedom my family granted me in all my work.

To lord Shiv for his blessings. To Krishna for bieng an amazing partner, and co-author.

Disclaimer: Don't be a blind devotee. Believe in yourself and the compassion of God, no matter what. I write this with the blessings of Lord Krishna (my beloved), the Eternal King who has been extremely compassionate to me.

Always remember beloved... Life and love never ends...

Prologue

This is a magical journey..written in love for his highness Lord Shiv.

From the fierce battle grounds of Afghanistan, to the shores of south India.

This work was originally started to rewrite the Shiv purana but it ended up as a mix

of both the ancient and the contemporary. The purpose of this book is to

bask into the glory of lord Shiv and his pastimes. To fall in love with him again and again.

THE GREAT BATTLE – AFGHANS AND THE LORD

Somewhere in the rocky terrains of Afghanistan, an icy cold wind was blowing. Dawn was approaching faster than the sounds of rustling feet and neighing horses in the distance. A caravan of British soldiers was carefully marching towards their camps. The colonel of the battalion raised his hat and shouted, "Come on soldiers, hurry up, or else we'll be late for supper. I am sure you don't intend to skip dinner as well."

"Aye aye Colonel Martin! We definitely don't want to miss the turkey today," chuckled one British soldier. Some Indian soldiers who knew English smiled as they wiped dust from their faces. Good food and wine is a soldier's delight.

"Sir ji, I know a place in Kabul where they serve delicious curry and chicken along with wine," said Raftar; he was an Indian sepoy from the Highlands.

"O really, then we ought to try some. Where is it?" asked Colonel Martin.

"Sir ji, it's somewhere near Lala's shop… you know, the one near Krishna Market."

"Oh sure, we'll take Banna along as well," the Colonel replied, smiling.

"Hey, how far is the camp post, Raftar" inquired Captain Turnbull as he unfolded the map.

Raftar wiped sweat off his forehead and said, "Just two kilometres sir," as he pointed towards a dusty mountain with a British flag mounted on the top.

As the sun set, the horses stealthily carried the arms and guns, treading on the mounds of sand.

"So George, did you get any news of your wife, I heard she was expecting?" asked Colonel Martin.

"No sir," replied George, a British sepoy. "Though I heard from her last week," he continued, blushing.

The horses suddenly started neighing louder, as if they could sense some danger. Colonel Martin's horse stopped with a thud.

Suddenly a spear shot through the wind and hit Raftar's hand. "Aaa," yelled Raftar in pain and shock as blood dripped down his arm.

"It's the Pathans, take your positions quick!" screamed Captain Turnbull who was already loading his rifle while crouching behind the horse.

Some Indian soldiers ran towards Raftar, whose hand was bleeding profusely, and tended to him. All of them were in shock.

"It's a trap. Run!" screamed another man.

Loud noises of soldiers and horses started coming in from all sides. In no time, Colonel Martin and his soldiers were surrounded by over a hundred Pathans.

George gulped his fear, and while the other soldiers were also scared, they kept faith in their brave hearts.

The Pathans' faces were covered with cloth, and they all had guns in their hands. Their chief emerged from the pack and smiled cunningly. "You have been surrounded by us. There is no way out. Surrender or die!" he said.

Turnbull turned to Martin in disdain. "Oh Jesus! Have mercy on us Lord."

"If we surrender, they will keep us as prisoners," whispered Martin in his ear.

"But we have only 50 soldiers," replied Turnbull.

"Don't doubt our valour, sir. We are not cowards. We will fight till the end and defeat these mice," said an Indian soldier.

"I don't doubt that but..." Martin paused for a bit. "Okay, go then," he finished and closed his eyes in prayer.

Meanwhile, the Pathans had been closing in slowly, just like a cat does with its prey.

Suddenly a cloud of dust blew in, and everything became less visible.

And from nowhere, a Hindu yogi appeared with a trishul (trident) in his hand.

He was a handsome man, about 25 years old with a strange aura around his face. Long braids hung down his shoulders with bhasma, a type of ash, streaking across his toned, muscular body and his broad shoulders. Oh those attractive, debonair looks would have stolen the heart of any fair maiden. Those strong manly eyebrows and lotus-shaped eyes were unforgettable... as was the third eye on a forehead decorated with a tilak. He smelled like sandalwood and was draped in lion skin and rudraksha mala.

"Stop or face my ire!" he yelled in Hindi as he hastened past the Pathans barefoot.

"And who are you?" asked the sardar of the troops.

"I am a friend," replied the strange yogi .

"Oh and what if we don't listen to you?" quipped another Pathan. "There are hundreds of us. Get out of our way," he shouted as he pointed his gun at the yogi's chandan-laced head.

The yogi jerked the gun and pointed the trishul towards his heart. His eyes looked red with anger.

"Shoot!" the sardar yelled. But the gun didn't work. Some Pathan soldiers ran towards him to subdue him. But the yogi leapt out of the way as the earth trembled in fear. He poked the trishul in one soldier's heart. Moving swiftly like a hungry tiger, he killed many more men with his trishul. The Pathans surrounded him with guns, but he used his trishul to fight with valour. In the process, his braids came undone. One Pathan tried to shoot him but he stopped the bullet with his fingers and killed him with his trishul. With his careful manoeuvring, neither their bullets nor their swords were able to pierce him. Seeing him fight alone with such bravery the British soldiers also gained courage. Gunshots rang out and dust blew up. The Indian soldiers took out their swords and guns.

Captain Martin shot the sardar in his leg. He fought very bravely. Raftar also managed a few shots with his wounded hand. Turnbull ended up with a sword wound on his hand and a few minor injuries. Some soldiers suffered gunshot wounds. They fought and fought till very few Pathans were left. The rest of the men fled.

At the end of it all, Colonel Martin thanked the yogi.

The yogi softly smiled and said, "Your wife is a devotee of mine. I am very pleased with her devotion. That is why I appeared to help you. You are my responsibility now. Come, let's go."

"My wife sir?" the colonel asked, confused.

"Yes, she often visits my temple and is very stressed about you." Although the colonel couldn't understand what he meant, he thanked him again. The men continued on their way and swiftly reached their post. The guards at the post welcomed them as the soldiers recounted the horrors of the battle. The wounded were tended to. Even in the moon light, the yogi's face shone with a beautifully dusky aura, making him look even more handsome. Colonel Martin led him to dinner. All around them, men made merry and enjoyed the delicious food the cook had prepared. The yogi was their saviour, and they all looked upon him with admiration.

"So sir, where do you hail from?" Captain Turnbull asked in Hindi .

Yogi smiled. "I am a Yogi. I never stay at a particular place. But I generally reside in Kailash."

"Oh, it's pretty cold out there," remarked Captain Turnbull. He was quite impressed with the man's valour.

"I thought it was my end today, but you saved us, yogi baba. You indeed were a miracle from god," said Raftar with gratitude in his eyes.

Mani the cook served more rotis to Captain Martin and his new yogi friend.

"You should have seen Mani, how valorous yogi baba was," Colonel Martin said. "How those Pathans were so scared when he fought like a tiger amongst a flock of sheep."

Baba smiled humbly.

"Really?" replied Mani enthusiastically. "Then babaji, please taste this rasgulla too; you have hardly eaten anything."

The yogi picked the rasgulla and tasted it. "It's delicious mmm... but all my valour fails in front of your cooking,"

Mani laughed merrily. "Oh you are too kind sir."

"Oh you should have seen how the sardar ran way like a scoundrel and how the others trembled with fear. He even stopped the bullets with his trishul," Colonel Martin continued.

"Really!" Mani exclaimed, "You must be a magician. So skilled in trishul. Where did you learn it?"

"It's just Shiva's grace," replied the yogi.

So the night passed merrily mood as people mingled with the great man. They were very tired from the day's battle, and thus they all slept swiftly after dinner.

In the morning, Captain Turnbull and Colonel Martin parted with the yogi after he gave them his blessings. He smiled at Colonel Martin and said, "Go to your wife and tell her your Shiva came."

Then a week passed since that incident.

Colonel Martin had reached home. Mrs Martin greeted him with a sigh of relief. "Oh honey, I'm so happy you are alright!" she exclaimed and hugged him.

"Love you honey," he said and kissed her on the cheek.

"Baby how have you been? I was so anxious for your letter."

"Oh yeah. You don't know what we have been through. God helped us, you know," said Colonel Martin as he removed his bag and kept it on the sofa.

"What happened? I also felt something fishy when I didn't get your letter. Here have some water," said Mrs Martin, handing him a glass of water.

"Thanks. The Pathans attacked us dear. Luckily a brave Indian yogi saved my life."

"Oh really! God blessed us indeed. Tell me all about it."

"A week ago, we were going to our new post when suddenly, we were surrounded by Pathans. It was so bad that there was no way to escape. I thought we were going to die. Suddenly, out of nowhere, this yogi came and fought valiantly with them. The Pathans were no match for him. Seeing him fight alone lifted our spirits as well, and we defeated them."

"Oh that's amazing!" I was so tensed and anxious that I prayed for you daily. I would go to the nearby Shiva temple and pray with full faith."

He smiled. "That's my sweetheart. Come, I'll thank your Shiva too."

The next day they visited the temple. "Namaste," the temple priest greeted them. "How are you madam? Is this your husband?"

"Yes panditji, meet Mr. Martin, my husband." She smiled and gave him the pious bel leaves typically offered to Lord Shiva and flowers brought for the prayer.

"All hale and hearty panditji," said Colonel Martin, smiling.

"I also prayed for your well-being sir. Your wife was so anxious about your letter," said the pandit as he handed him some prasadam (sweets blessed by the lord).

"Oh that was very kind of you," said Martin and smiled. "Hey wait!" he suddenly exclaimed on seeing the beautiful idol of Lord Shiva. "Honey that yogi looked exactly like this."

"What!" exclaimed Mrs Martin. She was startled as much as overwhelmed. Tears of faith rolled down her eyes.

"Really?" exclaimed the pandit with joy. "You truly are a great devotee, madam. Lord Shiva himself came to protect your husband."

Mrs. Martin hugged the Shiva Lingam again and again as tears rolled down her eyes. After all, her faith had been answered. Mr Martin stood with folded hands – faith in his eyes and peace in his heart.

"We are very lucky indeed. You, missy, are one lucky woman," he said as he lovingly hugged his wife and kissed her cheek.

Chants of "Har Har Mahadev! (Glories to Lord Shiva)" started in the background as the morning aarti started with loud beats of the damaru. That aarti felt special and ethereal to everyone present there that day – as if Lord Shiva was standing beside them. His smiling idol seemed more beautiful, as did the shining diamond-studded golden trishul in his valorous hands. It symbolized his protection and compassion for all those who sought his refuge.

CHAPTER TWO

THE UNUSUAL CUSTOMER AND THE BLESSED CONCUBINE

And now we come to a timeless tale... of beauty, passion and a compassionate heart. Of a demigod and his muse. A devotee and her lord. In a small village called Nandigrama there lived a girl called Mahananda. Born into beauty, wealth and talent, she was a harlot by profession, yet she was proficient at dance and music. She was a famous woman amongst the nobility and was often invited by kings and queens for her dances and songs. She was also deeply devoted to the great Lord Shiva and would often sing and dance for him. She would comb her hair like it was his. She would regularly bathe the Shiva Lingam and take care of it. When she would bathe herself, she would feel his presence in the water, soaking in the divine feelings of love for the lord. She would prepare sacred dances for his amusement. Mahananda would decorate herself with holy ash and would wear sacred rudraksha beads.

One day, deep in her devotion, she was dancing for the lord. Suddenly there was a knock on the door. She opened the door and saw a handsome man, presumably a customer. But it was Lord Shiva himself disguised as a handsome and wealthy merchant. He was anointed with ash and had beautiful matted hair. He was wearing bangles with beautiful gems around his wrists and diamond-studded gold earrings. Oh what passion shimmered in those kohl-laced eyes!

Mahananda, the beautiful one, received him with pleasure and seated him with reverence and honour. Seeing his beautiful jewels, the woman was charmed and desired to have them for herself. "Wow!" she exclaimed, "lovely ornaments... they are amazing."

"Oh these... you like them?" Shiva asked, smiling as he sensed her desire. "If you are so attracted to these splendid jewels, my dear, then I can give them to you... but you will have to pay a price for them?"

"Oh a price... hmm," she said and tickled his tummy, "Won't my charms be enough?

"I am a merchant. I don't mix passion with money." He smiled back.

"Good control, merchant. Not many can resist my charms. Prostitution is my family business. I am a courtesan, not a wife," she said in a sad voice. The soft-hearted lord gently cupped her chin and turned her face towards him. "Don't be sad... I don't judge. Be with me as my wife for three nights. I am a married man. I have to return home after my merchandise is sold. Then these gem-studded bangles will be yours, I promise. The sun and moon are our two witnesses. Repeat after me: Satya! Satya! Satya! (meaning "Truth")."

"My Lord, you weaken me with your kindness," she said.

"Now... touch my heart and embrace me," said the lord in a sensual tone.

She placed her hand in the hands of the handsome one and looked faithfully into his eyes.

"Oh Lord! I will satisfy your carnal desires... for three days and nights as your wife," she said and repeated the solemn promise with the sun and moon as her witness. After this she delightfully began to caress his hair, fondling his jewels and hugging Lord Shiva. She caressed his earrings and inhaled his fragrance... so delightful it was. The fragrance of a yogi – all sandalwood and rose.

"You sure smell good," she said. "You look so extraordinary in your simplicity."

Shiva blushed. "Here, take these gem-studded bangles." Then he took out a Shiva Lingam and handed it to her. "I am a great devotee of the lord," he said firmly. "This gem-studded lingam of Shiva is dearer to me than life itself. Hide it in the temple and keep it with care."

"Oh you're a devotee of the lord? I too am his follower." She touched the lingam to her forehead in obeisance and placed it in her dancing room. She cleaned the room and decorated the bed with roses and lit candles to create a romantic atmosphere for her wealthy customer. Soft petals lay on the bed but the softest was Mahananda herself. "O maiden... how charming you are... lucky are thou and so am I, such lovely decoration.

"Just for you, only on Mondays," she said, winking and kissing him passionately on his forehead (Monday is considered an auspicious day for worshipping Lord Shiva).

He wiped off the tilak on his head and removed his turban. He also removed her dupatta and as he kissed her bindi, she smiled and fell in love, there and then. Such paranormal lust... engulfed her heart. Such divinity was not a lie... it was something only a pure devotee experiences.

Romantic sophistications didn't seem to matter

as he caressed her hair like a lustful lover.
With a passionate jolt, he held her waist.
Those strong arms... "O' Lord,
make me thine slave," she said.
He happily kissed her gently and softly,
like a soft butterfly and a rose,
and a kiss that would forever change her life.
Lost in eyes that could seduce goddesses,
she removed his shirt.
And as they kissed and kissed even more,
Mahananda lost herself in him.
There was a whore no more –
just the lord and the chalice
for his lustful love.
Lost in passion that can control the universe,
she kissed him endlessly all over his waist and neck.
Even demigods may get jealous of a passion that could
stop time
"Be my bride for three days, what do you say?" he said
"You know I am a lonely traveller, I have to return home
after business."
"Don't speak of it," she said sadly, "I know."
"Some travellers don't return," he said and smiled
as she hid her face in his chest.
When he blushed with his clever eyes,
she blushed too, even in the winter cold,
Those strong arms held the happiness and passion of a
wife
when she meets her true master.
He caressed her hair and felt her pain.
The love she had yearned for over an eternity
was hers, but only for three nights.
It seemed that heaven was hers

and hell didn't matter.

She felt lucky to have been a slave of destiny,

but unlucky mostly because she was his wife at heart, but not in his destiny...

Her pure lips were humble, and so were her loving intentions –

to kiss him, to caress him, to take care of him

in every moment they spent together.

Her kisses mapped out his body and devoured his saintly pride.

Just know that god was there... to kiss her and make her his bride

Tears fell from her eyes,

falling on his shoulder, and he kissed them with his lips

Not many could have coped with his passion,

but she was lost in a desolate hope,

as if nothing seemed to matter, but this handsome merchant.

Just as she was his bride, he held gold in his hands

to shower on his wife for the night, but she smiled sadly,

because gold was not what she needed,

but just his sweet faithful smile...

And a promise that he'll be hers forever – even if it goes unfulfilled, even if it goes unfulfilled.

She took out the dagger from his pocket when he was kissing her breasts in passion and asked him, "What if I kill you?" He smiled and, kissing her hand romantically, took the knife and cut the winding threads of her choli. She blushed.

"Now you've killed me." He winked and smiled.

She smiled and said, "You naughty man," and nudged his nose. "You look like a swan."

"I know, but your breasts are beautiful. Let me touch them more," he replied naughtily.

"Oh, only if you can catch me," she said and chuckled.

She ran behind the curtains that he gently pushed aside.

As he was teasing her, she saw a beautiful bracelet on his arms.

"Wow!" she exclaimed, "that's a beautiful bracelet."

His unrefined love was like a raw wine,

and in their nakedness lay the fulfilment of souls.

His nectar descended into her womb,

as he removed the kajal from her kohl-laden eyes with his kisses.

In their lust blossomed the weakness of a harlot and the purity of a wife.

And in their bed the softness of the quilt, the coldness of the winter,

the soft pillows and the handsome merchant in guise of a passionate customer.

He kissed her navel and then moved slowly to her moonlit face,

with her lipstick colouring his lips,

with his curly locks entangled with hers,

and descended in the ocean of her heart.

The night passed in romance, and the days were just great.

She would make him food and take care of his needs like a wife.

She would comb his hair, bathe him and wait for him when he went away.

She cleaned him up when he came back – just like husband and wife.

With the lord in a courtesan's cottage,

with gold in his hand and love in his heart.

How Mahananda's soul dances in this cage (body) to please her lover's heart.

A sensitive man, an emotional heart

"My sweetheart, please me, oh lover, please me with your Art,

caress me with love, caress me with your truth

Who are you O' great saint?

Who are you O' great one?

Thine lotus eyes, I love...

Thine chiselled body, I wish to respect

by applying turmeric to cover your wounded heart."

"O my princess I love you though,

How may I caress thee?

What I may shower your body with first?"

Shiva: "Your body first..."

Mahananda: "Is that all you need?

Take my poetry, it is my soul."

Shiva: "All free? Ask for something big."

Mahananda: "My lover, you became a husband, what else can I ask for?

I yearned for one... if only for three days.

Girls like us can only dream of love.

Shivji has blessed me with your love...

O' Lord, take me as a servant in your house, so that I can serve you all my life."

Shiv smiled and said, "My beloved... I can shower you with gold and gems but I cannot stay here, for my wife longs for me at home. Moreover I have family responsibilities."

"Then give me a hug," she said with a sad smile.

The maid brought them tea and snacks.

"Here, you have," he said, lovingly handing her a snack, pleasing her with his eyes, understanding her pain.

"Thank you dear," said she, pouring tea in his cup.

"So do you want to go to the jewellery market today? Anything to please these sad eyes," the lord said.

Mahananda smiled and readily agreed.

They roamed the market that day and enjoyed their time together as a loving couple.

Next day, when Lord Shiva disguised as a merchant to go out for his merchandise, the lingam caught fire. The maid ran and alerted Mahananda who was combing her hair. The whole of the dancing room was on fire. The beautiful gem-studded lingam lay burning on the couch. Mahananda and the merchant ran towards the room. Seeing the lingam ablaze, the merchant started panicking. He tried to save it from burning but the scorching heat was too powerful; it burnt the lingam to ashes in no time. Tears rolled down the merchant's eyes. Mahananda tried to console him but he scolded her back. "You should have taken care of my lingam. Didn't I inform you earlier that it was more precious to me than life itself?"

Tears rolled down the harlot's eyes. The merchant was burning in the inferno of his anger. Unwilling to be budged by her tears, he said, "Light a pyre for me now. I will burn with it. My life is useless without my lord." Mahananda tried her best to console him. But he ordered the servants to light a pyre at the cremation ground.

An hour later, a pyre was laid out for the gentleman. The big cremation ground stood empty with one funeral fire burning at a distance. Some mourners also stood in silence. The merchant entered the crematorium with Mahananda, whose face was soaked in tears. The servants guided him to the funeral altar. The harlot again tried her best to stop him but to no avail. He held a fire baton in his hands and steadily lit the sacred fire at the altar. As the funeral pyre was burning, Mahananda ran towards the pyre just as the merchant was entering it. She fell on her beloved's lotus feet. "Please don't burn, my master... take my life instead. I was your wife for three days. Don't make me a widow or else I'll burn myself too."

"It's my duty to my beloved lord," he said with tears in his hurt, angry eyes and sat on the burning pyre. The courtesan Mahananda also sat on the pyre with him. "I will also sacrifice my life then, because it's my duty to follow my husband's path. You may die but our love shall not," she said fiercely and sat in a praying posture waiting for her body to burn, trembling with fear for her and her husband. As the fire steadily approached their bodies, Shiva hugged her tightly and resumed his divine form. Amongst the billowing smoke they looked like an amalgamation of coal and snow, like fireflies madly in love. Mahananda opened her eyes and was appalled.

She was being embraced by a handsome yogi with a snake around his neck, bhasma on his body, sacred rudraksha beads, a three-striped tilak and a third vertical eye on his forehead. A beautiful crescent moon sat atop his head, and he wore a necklace of gold.

The fire died down, and flowers appeared on the pyre.

She touched him and pinched herself. "I can't believe it!"

Shiva smiled and blushed.

"Oh my god! It's Shivji, the lord himself... Your grace," she said and fell at his feet. "Please forgive me, Lord," she said, trembling with fear. "I never realised it was you."

He cupped her lovely face in her hands and said, "You are no longer a prostitute. I am touched by your devotion, my darling. I assumed the form of a merchant to see you so I could test the firmness of your faith. I set the dance hall on fire and the lingam too, for this play of Lord. You became a sati for me; thus you have been cleansed and will be remembered as a revered devotee of mine. I am the provider of all materialistic desires and pleasures unattainable in the three worlds. There is nothing in this universe that can't be attainable." A teary-eyed Mahananda looked into his eyes lovingly and said "O Revered One! Only thine presence in my heart is necessary for my survival. I no longer seek any materialistic pleasures. After the touch of your lotus feet, all my selfish desires have left my mind. All my relatives are eager to come to you as I am. Please bless them all and take us all together to your heavenly abode. Salvation at your holy feet is all I need."

"You are no longer a prostitute... My beloved, come with me," and so saying, the slender one picked the girl in his strong arms while the servants chanted "Har Har Mahadev! Jai Shiv Shankar!"

They passionately kissed each other like two lovers dissolved in each other.. all the ego vanished, what remained was the compassionate lord and the blessed wife..

Thus Mahananda went to Shiva's heavenly abode on mount Kailash, and received eternal bliss at the side of his lotus feet.

Poem

This blazing fire
can't burn my heart to ashes
O handsome prince, why do you burn with me
when there's an oasis outside?
This heat is nothing compared to mine.
This rapid reaction,
this spontaneous oxidation
of my soul in lust for your body
In love, this sinful lust dissolves.

It's sinful but pure.
In nothingness my ego absolves,
Seeing you burn, my heart gets crushed
that you became mine only for three nights.
It was lust but in devotion.
A harlot and her mansion and a handsome knight
A divine crush, an unusual dream
that, this time, knows the magic of your love,
that in the touching of our bodies
lies the fulfilment of the souls.
In the entanglement of our legs and fingers
In the naked moment
The shame still comes like a lamp shining in the darkness,
in the unwinding of thine caresses,
What do these hypocrite priests know of my heart?
In different faces you came to me
A habitué of my bodily ends
You gave me heaven,
and I gave you a pyre.
Let's meet again in the highlands,
in fields covered in grapevines and trees,
in fields covered with winery,
Let's meet again, O' chastiser.
Hiding in a thousand bodies, but only one that's chaste

—

I as a concubine and you as my customer.

CHAPTER THREE

THE PRINCESS WHO BECAME A YOGINI...

Her beautiful hair decorated with flowers, with a sweet smile on her face.

Draped in a saree, still waiting for her soulmate, like a mermaid in the sea.

Lord Shiva: with love in her heart and lots of pain, it's still Shiva who waits, beloved... it's still me... Meet me again in solitaire, silly girl, what do you wait for in the sea?

One winter morning, the large waves of the sea splashed on the shore, washing the footsteps of the children who would play on the beach. Loud temple bells from a distant Shiva temple rang out behind the huts. Bullocks grazed near the courtyard of the chief priest's house. Nearby was the great palace of the king. The sun shone bright as a young princess Kanya Kumari appeared on the shore with her friends; she was draped in a sari with a golden border. She was the princess of the southern kingdom. Her friends called her Kanya. She was a devotee of Lord Shiva.

She had a beautiful shining face haloed in a mystic aura – beautiful brown almond-shaped eyes, long hair that fell in curls and was adorned with jasmine and rose, doe-like ears... oh! what a beauty. Golden earrings hung from her soft earlobes, and a shining little bindi dotted her forehead. She wore a golden pendant that had a rudraksha attached to it (as a symbol of devotion to Lord Shiva). She was accompanied by her friends and maids.

"O Kanya!" said one of her friends as she came running to the princess, "look I have found a conch shell." Kanya Kumari was taking a bath in the water with some other girls. "Hey, Supriya, Kanya Kumari, Antara come look... there's a nutmeg here as well." Kanya was delighted at the shells. She came swimming to the beach and took the shell from her friend.

"Wow! They are beautiful. I'll make garlands for Shiv Ratri (a festival celebrating the wedding of Lord Shiva)." She collected some more conch shells and nutmegs that had washed on the shore. "Hey give it to me," said Supriya. "I'll make one for you, sister." They changed clothes and sat down to make a necklace. "I have some pearls," said Kanya, "let's add them to the necklace as well." Antara took a needle and sewed the pearls together. "Look, how beautiful!" she exclaimed as she showed it to everyone. "Aww! They look so elegant. Let's wear them," said Kanya. So the princess wore them. "Wow! You look beautiful princess," exclaimed a maid.

"Oooh, decorating yourself for lord, huh! Lest the handsome Shiva cast an eye on you," teased Supriya. "Oh come on now, it's not for him okay, I mean why would he cast an eye on me?" said the beautiful Kanya Kumari, blushing and avoiding her friends' teasing glances. "Look how she's blushing like a bride," said her friend. "No no no, not her again. It's Monday and my lucky day. Today, instead of Shakti, he'll bestow his kindness on me," said Antara, winking.

"Oh come on, he won't even look at you. Mahadev doesn't cheat," said the jealous Kanya. "Yeah, we'll see. I bet you 15 gold coins. He will stary when I wear my embroidered veil and my lehenga. He'll fall for my beauty at once," teased another one of the girls.

"Okay, don't cast an evil eye on the lord. You'll corrupt her innocent Shiva with your guiles," said Sukanya, laughing.

He has no preferences for skeletons like you, you shallow people! thought an angry and sad Kanya Kumari. Suddenly the bells of the temple rang through the village. The aarti of Shiva had begun. "Oh come on girls, let's hurry. Here, take the basket," she said, handing the pooja basket to the maids. The girls hurried to the temple with the maids. Kanya ran ahead so as to not be late for the pooja. As they were hurrying, Kanya tripped and fell down the slimy stairs of the hill where the temple was located. She sat there crying. "Oh! Gauri-Shankar," she wailed, referring to another one of Lord Shiva's names.

Her leg ached terribly but there was nobody around to help. A helpless Kanya began to look around for help. Suddenly a warm hand held her hand. "May I help you lady?" said a sweet manly voice. She looked behind.

A young man with a turban and golden-bordered white dhoti stood before her. He was handsome with a charmingly gentle demeanour. She felt an unusual attraction towards him. He wore rudraksha and had a three-striped tilak on his forehead. "Oh what are you thinking?" he asked. The princess blinked and blushed. "Sorry... I just tripped. My friends have moved ahead. I have to reach the temple for the pooja." "Gosh! these stairs are slippery," said he, looking around. "My name is Bhola, and I am the son of the priest," he said. Little did the princess know that it was

Lord Shiva himself. He held her by the shoulder and made her sit on the rock. "Here, I'll give your leg a slight twist; it's a simple sprain, so it'll be fine." "Alright," said Kanya Kumari. He twisted her ankle and massaged her soft feet with his fingers. Then the handsome one looked into her eyes. "Feeling better? he asked.

"Yes, thank you," she shyly said.

"Does it hurt?" he asked

"It's better," she said, smiling and wiping the tears from her eyes.

"Try to get up," he said, extending his hand. "Come I'll pick you up."

She hesitated a bit, not trusting an unknown stranger.

"It's okay, don't worry. I am going the same way. If you feel comfortable..." he said gently.

"Umm..." She was mulling over his offer.

"Oh I am late for prasadam. I am going," he said as he looked up in a hurry.

"Wait! wait! Sorry, my friends must have already reached the temple."

He reassured her that she'll be safe and picked her up in his arms.

She smiled and looked at him admiringly. He blushed under her adoring gaze.

"So you look like you're from a noble family," he said.

"Without doubt sir. I am princess Kanya Kumari."

"Oh!" the man replied, smiling. "So you are here for the pooja, hmm... no maids?"

"They have left long ahead."

"It's okay, you are safe with me, lucky maiden," he said and winked. *Handsome flirt!* thought Kanya Kumari. Soon it started raining. They both had to take shelter under a leaky cave. "It's cold here," said Kanya, shivering. "Let me warm you up. Here, collect some twigs." So saying, he took out some flint stones from his pocket as Kanya collected dry twigs and branches. They lit a fire together. He looked at her beautiful dishevelled hair and moon face. She too looked at him through the corner of her eyes, pretending that she did not see. "Hey look, a taro plant!" Bhola exclaimed. "Yeah, let's make a umbrella with this," she chirped happily. The sober-natured Bhola tied the ends of the large taro leaves and made an umbrella. They chatted amicably for some time.

What is heaven compared to that moment? A handsome yogi and a beautiful princess – blossoming of youth... with hearts so naïve. With a brave demigod so gentle and suave, one would forget all their wealth. For if we have good company, we can be happy even in a cave... That one hour was blissful. Shiva made the sweet princess laugh with his jokes. Her injured leg had almost healed. After the rain subsided to a slight drizzle, they took out their taro leaf umbrellas and walked to the temple. With Kanya in his warm arms, the touching of their bodies set off complex reactions. Their eyes played hide and seek, while a naughty smile graced his dimples. When they reached the courtyard of the temple, Kanya gave him her pearl necklace with conchshells and nutmegs as a parting gift. He smiled and said, "We are eternal travellers who shall meet again soon." He kissed her forehead and left. The princess softly smiled and blushed. After he left, she went into the temple. The priests were chanting hymns outside in the courtyard, whilechants of Har Har Mahadev! rang out in the background as the morning aarti had finished. The temple hall was empty inside. Shiva's idol seemed more beautiful with the shining aura and trishul in his strong muscular hands. *Don't make me feel weak in these arms, O' Handsome one*, thought Kanya Kumari.

Suddenly her eyes halted on his chest, where her pearl necklace with conchshells and nutmegs adorned his neck. Tears fell from her eyes. She realised that it was Mahadev who had come to her rescue as Bhola. In a rush of emotions, she hugged Lord Shiva's idol in gratitude. And as she was hugging the lord's idol, he moved and smiled. "Hey, don't cry dear." Kanya was dumbfounded. The lord assumed his divine form with a lotus in his hands. When he came near her, her heart started beating faster than it should. A numbness pooled in her nerves. He came nearer and nearer, closer and closer. Time stood still. His aura radiated everywhere. "Bless you, dear devotee," he said. "Ask for anything you want. I am pleased with your simplicity and devotion." The beautiful Kanya Kumari blushed. "What shall I ask of you, lord?"

"I know what is in your heart. You were an incarnation of Para Shakti (a goddess) who was born on earth as a human, to punish the evil and wicked," he said.

She almost fainted at the revelation, eventually accepting the truth. He calmed her in his arms. He then asked for her hand in marriage: "I fell for your beauty and devotion; thus I would like to ask for the maiden's hand in marriage." Kanya Kumari couldn't believe her ears. She agreed readily. "I'll marry you next month, cheer up my bride... your groom will wait," the lord said and kissed her forehead, smearing her tilak. Kanya closed her eyes and kissed him back. After that, she touched his feet.

He playfully nudged her nose. The princess smiled and blushed red like a bride. "Wait for me on the shore for devi pooja (prayer day); we shall meet in the evening to discuss the matter," said he. The princess nodded with tears of gratitude in her eyes. Soon the lord disappeared. All her friends came running towards her. Sukanya looked very worried. Her mother also came running. "Where were you Kanya?" she angrily asked. "Yes, we were searching all over for you. Queen Mother was so worried," said Antara. Kanya Kumari told them all about the incident and about Lord Shiva's proposal. Then a strong aura emanated from the lord's idol, confirming the truth.

"That is the truth! But o' mother, not without your acceptance. Please be kind enough to accept my humble proposal to this beautiful princess," the lord said, appearing in his divine form. The angels played divine conch music to herald his presence. He held the hand of her father and asked for the bride's hand. Seeing the lord himself, the king was overwhelmed. He hugged his son-in-law. "It must have been the pious deeds of our ancestors that you yourself have proposed our daughter. We are humbled lord," he said with tears in his eyes. Lovingly, the compassionate lord wiped tears from his eyes, touched his feet and took his blessings.

"Prepare for the ceremony, my great king, for your daughter is mine from now. I will marry her a month from now."

The king agreed. The palanquins waited outside, and so did the horses. The queen and king were delighted. Temple bells rang out joyously. All the maids congratulated her. Her friends hugged her – some with love and some with envy.

<u>Poem</u>

What pain it is
in this love, my darling?
In the sensuousness of your caresses,
my heart breaks like a drop of rain
and like a drop, let me mix in your ripples.

The desires of your fingers...
O yogi! I know you yearn for me.
Play me like a sitar in your hands
or like a flute in your hands.
It will break if you play it with ego.
Instead, play it with the softness of your pride.
Lost in my memory with a song,
I'll be there for my beloved's presence –
to feel his lotus feet, to wash them with my tears.
Shiva: "I'll comb your hair, why do you resist?
I'll decorate your hair, put flower pins in your hair bun
and cuddle your curls.
Let's embrace our love."
Kanya: "Then feel my breath, feel your tears and my
helplessness
that I learnt to rejoice in."
Shiva: "Then feel my kiss, or I'll hiss."
Kanya: "Stand by me, lucky tiger, oh my handsome
snake.
Let me submit to your desires
with a kiss of conjugal love.
Drink me like a wine or devour my nectar like a bumble
bee
for I am the honey of joy and rekindled hope
Soon we shall reunite, like the yin and yang
to dissolve in the elixir of life.
I'll care for your children, and your tantrums I will cope
with
When you will be my lord and I will be your wife..."
The blossom of romance passed soon. The day of engagement arrived. Shiva and Kanya were dressed elegantly. The maids stood with ceremonial lamps in their hands, as Shiva held Kanya's hands, and they celebrated the

ritual of engagement. Cupid's arrows hit the tender spots of the lovers' hearts. This beautiful couple felt grateful to god for their impending union. After the engagement ceremony, the guests had left, their relatives had gone to sleep. Without letting anybody know, they both went upstairs for fresh air.

Lord Shiva was in a romantic mood that day. Kanya was shy. She looked lovingly at him with her lotus eyes. The moon was in full bloom, while the sea waves softly crashed into the shore. The girl's heart beat fast as he came closer and closer. The cool air blew her long dark hair as he caressed the locks with his fingers. "Don't worry," he said, "I won't do anything." They looked into each other's eyes in conjugal love and devotion, both blushing. He touched her hands softly.

Then he fondled her bangles with his fingers. He clasped her hands as the moonlight shone on their angelic faces. His soft lips touched hers as they kissed each other without the fear of infamy. She shyly hugged him. It was the nectar of youth that brought their loving hearts together. Beneath the moon and the stars they stood gazing each other. It felt that he was her zenith and she was a star – as if the happiness of all the three worlds lay at his lotus feet, in a single, soft hug. He smoothly touched her waist, and Kanya felt too weak to resist. She felt safe in his arms; that moment was hers and his. Nobody could take it away.

He softly kissed her diamond engagement ring that glowed in the moonlight. Kanya blushed, and her heart beat faster. That night, they just hugged each other like two flowers blossoming in the rain, celebrating in the false hope of their reunion. Cupid also blushed with them.

But cruel as destiny was, the dark angels cast an evil eye on the innocuous couple.

When the divine sage Narada heard about this engagement, he spread the news amongst the gods. The message quickly spread like wildfire. Then the demigods realised that the princess was an incarnation of goddess Shakti who was destined to kill the demon Banasura. But there was a curse in this story: She had to be unmarried to kill the demon Banasura for whom she had incarnated as the human princess. So a plan was hatched by the demigods to hijack the bridegroom's party – the innocent Shiva who was preparing for the wedding ceremony.

The sage Narada appeared in the court of the king, claiming that it was a conspiracy of the demons that were pretending to be Shiva. Kanya's father was scared. He consulted the priests who suggested that the groom should bring things that could not be found anywhere on earth: A coconut without eyes, a sugarcane without joints and a betel leaf without veins.

Lord Shiva readily agreed and easily fulfilled this demand. Thus, the wedding date was decided. Soon the wedding day arrived. Dressed like a bride from a fairy tale, the young princess waited for her knight, her heart fluttering like a nightingale caught in the storm of a maiden's lust. Lord Shiva was dressed up like a handsome groom with sparkling danglers and diamond rings. His followers gave away alms to ward off the evil eye from the handsome groom.

The lord came in his royal attire.
like an iceberg that dissolves,
in one look of the lord's eyes
like a mountain clad in snow
like a leopard ready to seduce its prey
like a cupid's arrow ready to strike.

He set off from Kailash on his horse, with maids and servants riding behind with gifts for the bride. They travelled all day and night. When they reached the bride's village, the sage Narada falsely made the rooster crow, creating an illusion of dawn breaking. In Hindu marriages, if the groom's party doesn't arrive at the auspicious moment, they have to return. Thinking that he had missed the auspicious moment of the marriage, the priest declined to wait and left. The groom was left in agony and pain. The world seemed still. All of his sweetheart's dreams had been shattered. Knowing her destiny was to remain unmarried, Shiva returned to Suchindram. In his anger, he went deep in meditation.

On hearing the rooster, Kanya's parents were heartbroken. The auspicious time of marriage had passed, and the groom was nowhere to be seen. The bride was left in tears that night.

The pain of a heartbreak is hard to bear... alas there is no medicine for it. Even death cannot take away the grief of a broken heart. A bride waiting for her bridegroom and her lover was left in anguish.

Shattered into pieces, she cried all night and threw away her jewels in anger. The maids tried to console her but she didn't budge. She burnt everything that night, including the clothes, sweets and jewels. Rice and other grains kept for the wedding feast remained uncooked. She broke all her utensils and shattered her glass bangles. But it was not glass that broke that day – it was a soul that broke.

Kanya: "In his heart lies a cruel mistress,
my heart broke with a rooster's croak,
and my love didn't come."
Shiva: "For you didn't see, for you couldn't feel
the heart that broke with the dawn."

Kanya: "O beloved, what may I say?
how much I love you still
how I cried when your heart broke.
Leave all pride, and come to my arms.
Remove this ego's crown."
Shiva: "My beloved, the strings of my heart are broken still.
It's okay, love forgets love... with time, the wound heals.
Kanya: I'll touch your beating heart in earnest and cry
with my broken heart. Who said we are two?
We are one indeed.
I love you still; it's I who need
to enclose your eyes in the blink of mine
to feel how soft a man you are inside,
to kiss your tears... of that night and beyond.
So loving you are, so filled with love.
Let's be each other's canvas and paint our bodies.
Paint me as being lost in your conjugal love.
Come let's unite in a dance; fight with me first.
Make me win or I'll make you lose.
Submissive in my strong desires, I'll still make you blush.
Shiva: "I'll defeat you in a second
My beloved wife, but you are so pure that I may not defile.
I still burn in ashes of the fire you lit.
Dying alone every second, as a husband burning for his wife."

Poem

Helpless when you smile my Lord,
I fell for you the moment I met you.
O breaker of hearts, O handsome one,
those conchshells, those shy eyes

that fell in love the moment we met...
In that hall, there was silence
just you and me... and love.
With pain in my heart, and years of endless waiting,
I will still wait for you, my lover
life after life, birth after birth
with these flowers in my hand
and a lamp of hope in my heart
for that happiness of reunion.
In life we might not unite or maybe we shall,
when your passionate lover will be yours.
That day I shall rejoice,
for you were mine
always mine...
Shiva: "Not yet my lover, and yet no more...
these years of endless wait I have suffered my sweetheart
as him, as her and as both."

Her heart was thumping fast. As the waves of the sea dashed hard against the rocks, she put on the simple clothes of a yogini and decided to do penance for her beloved lord.

A heartbroken Kanya Kumari focused on her penance for her Lord Shiva. Meanwhile, the demons gained supremacy over the demigods, and unrighteousness began to spread like a disease. The demon king Banasura was protected by a sacred boon: He could be killed only by a virgin girl. One day, all hell broke loose in heaven, when Banasura attacked the demigods. There was bloodshed everywhere, and the demigods were driven away. The demons also tortured the sages and priests.

The heartbroken goddess had become a yogini to perform austerities for her beloved lord. The story of her broken marriage and her beauty reached Banasura. The guru of the demons also advised him to marry her so that he could subdue her as a wife. Thus, Banasura decided to propose to her. But as the sacred saying goes, one often meets his destiny on the path taken to avoid it.

One day near the seashore, as the beautiful lass performed her penance, demons surrounded her.

She opened her peaceful eyes. "Who are you, brothers?" she asked.

The demon king stood in the midst of his servants, disguised as a handsome king. "Allow me to introduce you to his highness," said one of the demons, as the demon king walked close to her. She became scared and nervous.

"The conqueror of the realms, the great king of heaven comes in his kindness, to propose to the beautiful princess of south, to take her as his wife."

Overconfident in his luck, the demon king proposed to her thus: "I am the great demon king. O beautiful princess, I have heard a lot about your beauty and your infamous marriage with Lord Shiva that couldn't be completed. In order to protect your honour," he cleverly continued, "I would like to marry you and take you as my wife."

"I am sorry to displease such a merciful king," she replied, "but I am a yogini for my beloved Lord Shiva." *Such an arrogant fool*, she thought to herself. Banasura persisted, trying to persuade her, till he became angry. "You filthy maiden," said he in lust and anger, "I will force you to be my bride." He then resumed his scary demon form and pulled her by her hair. Kanya Kumari was badly humiliated and maddened in anger. "Then suffer your punishment, you monster," she screamed in rage.

By the mercy of Lord Jagannath, the great goddess assumed her divine four-handed form. She held a divine discus (Sudarshana Chakra) in one hand and a trishul in the other. He attacked her, but she was strong and wild with anger. Her valour broke his manly pride, while she broke his sword. The monster looked at her in disbelief. Just then, the brave woman decapitated him with the Sudarshana Chakra. Moments before his death the evil one realised that the woman before him was Shakti, the great goddess herself. Overcome with terror at the great woman's power, he prayed for her mercy. She cooled down and forgave him by absolving his sins after his death. The great goddess still resides in a temple, the Devi Kanya Kumari temple, in Kanya Kumari, Kerala, India. After Banasura's defeat, the merciful lord and Kanya Kumari reunited in his heavenly abode.

Poem

No matter how endless this wait,
it is just a play of souls, a game.
It is in the purity of your love,
it is your smile that I fell for
it is just your sweet smile I wept for.
Our physical bodies may have been separated,
yet I reside in you, my husband, and as your innumerable wives
in innumerable lives.
Ah, this pain, it is so sweet still.
I still love you, I am still yours.
Your beauty touched me as the clothes I wear.
Your lips adorned me as the flowers I wear.
On my naked body, as I bathe
On my cloaked soul, as I pray
This sunshine touches you... and me
I feel it on my body, and thus we make love
in the rain that touches all in love and faith.
There is pain still, but I learnt to cope.

I learnt to laugh with you in my heart.
For your mermaid waits still on the shore.
O lord, innumerable are thine names
Who should I worship when thee reside in my heart?
When everything is you, you and just you...

CHAPTER FOUR

EVERYONE HARPS THERE IS NO TIME

I walked through the spur of the great Mount Kailash, observing the snowline on the top. It was a beautiful trek through the pine and deodar trees. It was the summer holidays, and I had saved some money for the holy Kedarnath yatra. It was the last day of the trek, and it was really cold! I had taken a Sherpa with me as a guide. I walked slowly and the journey was tough but I took Lord Shiva's name to gain courage. I enjoyed camping and had fun around the bonfire. My Sherpa and I sang hymns of the lord and cooked some daliya on our bonfire for the rest of the journey. I rented a pony for half the way. The trip was going fine, and I had soon taken lots of pictures. I was enjoying my journey, thanks to the blessings of Bholenath (another name for Lord Shiva). Suddenly the pony tripped and fell on the icy path. My bag and other belongings all fell into a deep trench. I felt a chill through my spine. Luckily the pony survived.

"Sir, are you okay," asked the guide who owned the pony.

"Phew! What a close call! I am okay. I hope the pony is fine."

"No sir, it has a leg injury," replied the guide with a sad face. "It won't be able to move any further."

"My bag, oh my bag! Did you see my bag?" I exclaimed.

"Yes sir, I saw it falling down the trench," replied the guide, looking a bit worried.

I looked down the trench and saw that it was rather deep and dark.

"Oh my god!" I exclaimed. I was stuck midway. The pony was injured, and my mobile and wallet were all gone. "Sir, don't worry, the journey is almost over, just two kilometres away is the Kedarnath temple. I won't take any money," the guide said kindly. "You can go on foot. It's just a straight path." So I got up and decided to complete my trip. It was noon. I walked along the rocky path, as several families went past me.

I was terribly tired, broke and drenched with sweat. Yet, at the same time, I felt feverish due to the cold. The cold wind blew my hair on my face. At last, I reached the Kedarnath temple. Dusk was starting to settle around me. Most of the people had left, so there were very few people around. I scrambled up the path with the help of a stick. My clothes were dusty, and so was my face. As I neared the gates of the temple, I saw the priest closing down the doors. I ran towards the temple. "Pujariji (priest)!" I said, "please let me inside!" As the priest peeped from the window, I shouted, "I have come from very far off."

The priest was already tired from the day's work. "Sorry son, today is the last day of closing, the temple will open after six months now." And then the priest went off. "Six months!" I exclaimed, heartbroken and depressed. The frost had got the better off me. Suddenly, it started raining. I hid in a small shed of the temple. No vehicle was around. It was freezing cold. The rain had worsened the cold. It had also grown dark.

When the rain subsided, I was too weak to walk back. I slept in the dark, waiting for nightfall. Suddenly, a handsome yogi appeared. He had dark brown matted hair, and his face was surrounded by a strange aura. He held a lamp in one hand and a trishul in another. "Get up Vatsya (devotee)," he said, holding my hand and helping me stand up. The strong-armed one smiled and said, "Who are you dear? And why are you lost at this time in this lonely place?"

I smiled and said, "Babaji, I am a devotee. I lost all my money and belongings when my pony collapsed on the way." The kind one smiled and gave me some food. I was delighted and gobbled it all up. The yogi smiled lovingly. He put a blanket around my body. I chatted with that yogi to pass the time. We talked about my life and about philosophy. We sang devotional songs and hymns. When we got ready to sleep, he blessed me, saying, "Don't worry son, you will get to visit the idol in the morning."

I was pacified and slept in the blanket he had given me. When I got up in the morning, the yogi was nowhere to be seen. I opened my eyes and saw a lot of people walking towards the Kedarnath temple. The weather had suddenly changed. Green grass had suddenly appeared everywhere, as if spring had already arrived. I was confused. The priest of the temple came outside to get some prayer stuff from the store room. I followed him inside. He looked at me and smiled. "Oh I know you. Aren't you the same guy who came six months ago? I am so sorry I couldn't be of any help that night."

"Oh pujariji, what are you saying?" I was confused. "Babuji, I just slept here all night."

"No dear, six months have passed since we last met," replied the confused priest.

I told him about the whole night and about the yogi as well.

The priest was surprised at the whole incident. Soon he realised what had happened. He fell to the floor in a deep bow, and with tears of faith in his eyes, he said "Vatsya, it was Lord Shiva himself who came to meet you. He is also the lord of time. He took you six months forward into the future so that you could see him today." Tears of happiness rolled down my eyes, and I ran inside the temple only to be awestruck with the strong aura emerging from the Shiva Lingam. I fell down at the feet of Shiva's idol. I was overwhelmed. There was divine light all around. All the devotees were overwhelmed by this miracle of the lord. The chants of "Har Har Mahadev!" grew louder and louder as the words resounded in the hearts of all his devotees. They symbolized his exceptional compassion to all those who come under his refuge.

<u>Poem</u>

Oh my lord beloved,
How innocent is thine smile
How lovely and soft you are
like the petals of a rose.
How merciful and kind thee are
like poetry and I your prose.
You loitered in the dark nights
on the mountain alone, O beloved of mine.
To keep me safe in the winters of my life.
I am useless, unworthy, O great lord,
but you saved my life.
You took me through an odyssey
through the winters of time.

The soft caresses of the beats of thy heart
I still feel in my heart.
I couldn't be your lover; I couldn't be your maiden
And that I still regret... but now all I want to be
is a humble person,
to lie in nothingness at your feet
to feel how humble my lord is...to feel thine sweetness,
the nectar of thine lips
to feel what a great prince you are...
<u>I CAN FEEL YOU'RE HEART BEATS</u>
POEM: NOT YET NO MORE ..
In this Infinity of time my lover..
I am you and still infinite
I love you as her touch
I touch you as the sun every day
in the cold wind that blows I feel you're breath
as if I am close so close that only you' re soul can be
I feel you as the river you bathe in
I feel you as a soul,
you are the heart in me..
that it beats for me, for me and just me
for I am one and yet nothing.. yet nothing
That's how I lie in everything in your arms my love
I'll meet you again, as we part sometimes
to reunite again in the rain
like the pure pelting of the snow
like the pure droplets of your tears my sweetheart
like the divine conjugality of our hearts
that fool never understand..
the oneness of our souls
the oneness of our breath
and how in infinity my true love
that you are like a thread my darling

and I thine pious beads, my rosary
the distances are of the heart..
O' beloved how may I tell
that I fell like a leaf into you' re arms
You're clever eyes and you're naughty ways
you're curly hairs and you're strong arms.
I love to feel weak in you sweetheart
let me cuddle you and jump into you're warmth
I don't touch my love for I may disrespect
I don't cross my love for they may not understand
how in its finity that's it's not that long
I have already united with you love as her
that its his will still that in resilience I accept
Shiv: softly smiles and says
come closer to my lips and cuddle me thus
fair enough they say, that we are still together
not yet no more..

not yet no more..

This is a true story of a girl named Swati. She was 22 years old with long straight hairs. Her eyes were speckled and she was fair in colour. She was a schizophrenic, It's a condition in which you see illusionary people. She was a bright student, pursuing her studies in medicine. Loneliness and stress had got the better of her. Who knew in her greatest despair would come the greatest blessing.

It was a lonely winter night, Swati was diagnosed with an unusual illness called schizophrenia. Her dad was extremely upset that day so he gave her an old rudraksha as a protection charm. It was a beautiful amulet with a rudraksha that had a natural shivling attached to it. As the days of her treatment passed, she felt very lonely. She was beautiful and well educated but no guy wanted to be in a relationship with a schizophrenic girl, most boys she came across were only interested in using her. The world felt numb for her. The days were dull and so were the nights. Every day passed like an year. She felt as if there was nothing left to live for. No hope for a bright future, no hope for a decent living.

Schizophrenic monsters harassed her day and night. One day she decided to meditate on lord shiv for peace. In order to gain Lords mercy she read the maha mritunjaya mantra 1000 times. It attracted the kind lord's attention.

One night she was sleeping in her night gown, suddenly she heard a knocking on the door.

She looked outside, She was baffled to see Lord shiv outside in her balcony. He was beautiful. Looking like a handsome peacock in the moonlight. Dressed up elegantly like a prince. Swati's eyes were dumbstruck to see such a handsome man in her balcony.

Who are you Sir? She asked as curiosity and fear got the better of her.

Don't be scared Swati, It's me Shiv.

I have come to meet you today due to you're pious devotion.

WOW! she exclaimed. Is it really the great Lord Shiv?

Tears welled up in her eyes.

Shh.. he said you might wake others..

They looked into each other's eyes. There was a lot of love in his heart, something the words could not describe..

The night had grown dark, it was very cold too. They sat down in the balcony and chatted for a while.

He caressed her hairs.. So how are you doing my love. I hope you are fine?

Swati smiled sadly I am okay, just the delusions getting worse. She hugged him close.

It's very painful. Do you have any medicine for this disorder? she naively asked.

"I do but you will have to be my maid first" he cleverly smiled.

"I will do anything sir, it's getting worse by day."

You will have to climb mount Kailash first, then I will gift you the medicine. He said seriously.

"Okay" she said still overwhelmed and happy at heart.

"See you at the park, you have to train for the mountain" said he "Brave girl" he laughed at heart.

Next morning the poor girl started exercising for her mountain training. The lord would lovingly make her do sit ups and various exercises every day.

1,2,3,4,...30..eh! I am soo tired lord shiv can I stop she asked lord in her mind.

"No not yet do till 50" he said in a stern voice noddingly.

She did the crunches till she was weary and drenched much to the amusement of lord.

"It was only to get her body to exercise so that she could recover from schizophrenia in reality".

She was not allowed outside her house so she couldn't visit temple.

Thus Swati made Shivlings of mud and would pour water on it every day to pray. She would bring flowers and Bel patra leaves to adorn the muddy shivling every day. Thinking that she might reach the dimension of Shiv after her death.

"So my love when will you climb the mountain for me" he asked one day.

"I will come dear when you will cross the mountain of ego, for mountains of ego are the toughest ones to be crossed by men of valour." She philosophically said.

We will unite Swati said he "like a butterfly when you will dance for me, like a sunshine in the rain, only to commence as a rainbow of my soul".

The lord had fallen in love with the girl. He was kind and decent to her as she was very naïve and loving. He would devote songs to her, make jokes to make her smile. He would write passionate poems and scare her as her as a possessive boyfriend if she ever talked to a wrong guy.

They wrote silly poems with each other to pass their time. He would make an imaginary cave for her and act like he was meditating in it. Come inside Swati he would call her in.. lovingly.

When she would run away he would catch her in his long braids.. to tease her lovingly.

In the sunshines of winter morning she would comb her hairs as if they were his braids.

She would dance for him sometimes. In her spare time, she wrote stories and poems for him out of devotion and love. To pamper him as lord is hungry for love only.

One day when Swati was checking out songs on her laptop, Lord lovingly came in front of her and started dancing like a peacock. He looked so beautiful as if nothing more beautiful existed. Blessed were these eyes that saw this dance.

Poem:
He danced like a peacock
a peacock in the rain
like a lotus petal
submissed sans his vain
So pure as a dew
he dances for a chosen few
his eyes O' mercy
can kill any.. even gods danced for thee

Thus I did resist
for In this silly form of mine, like the endless divine
I am very naïve and guile
to keep you pure
for my sweetheart you're still so pure that I may not defile
you're still so pure that I may not defile..
So pure is the nectar of you' re worship
but I will not Insult you again
for In this divine temple of mine
for you still dwell
for you still dwell
God: You're dancing eyebrows, you're crazy ways
still dwell in my heart O' Beloved
In his heart still reside
In the pure one, the formless one
The one sans ego and pride
Such love dwells in his heart.

With passing of time, Swati's condition worsened due to her schizophrenia. Due to the side effects of the medicine, life was getting worse. She requested Lord Shiv "Please take me to you're realm, in you're strong arms O' handsome one."

Lord Shiv jokingly said "Ok.. If you'll wait at 5 AM in the morning in the park I shall come to take you as my bride".

Swati smiled and said okay love I will wait for you jaan, but please come.

Next day she packed her bagpack for kailash with her toothbrush and garments.

She sat under a tree waiting for her dear lord.

She waited and waited till the sun came over. He showed his image in the sky.. but didn't take her to his abode. Swati was disappointed and heartbroken. At night, she lay crying on the bed.

Lord Shiv came close to her and hugged her in her bed. In her breast his heart was beating along with hers (A real paranormal experience). Swati smiled at lord's chivalry and cuteness.

Lord Shiv in his humility showed his beating heart in hers. To make her feel special he hugged her tight to kiss away her pain. In that one hug transcendental feelings entered her heart. She went into a state of spiritual ecstacy, their souls united at that moment. She hugged Shiv and went to sleep. Lord Shiv also lay beside her, subdued in divine love. It was heavens nectar and an eternal joy to unite with him, no matter how transient it might be.

As time passed her condition detiorated to the extent that it became unbearable for her. Each day was passing at god's mercy. She decided to end her life as she was eager to meet her beloved lord Shiv in his realm.

She was shit scared. "Are you giving up that easy" he calmly said.

"Yes lord I can't bear with this pain" said she with tears in her eyes.

"I will take you in my realm, but if you truly love me you won't do anything stupid " he said

that was the last time they talked so lovingly.

She was nervous and shit scared. She got detached to everything. Stopped eating. Her relatives were worried seeing such drastic depreciation in her health.

One day she mustered up courage and gobbled up 26 sleeping pills, enough to kill an elephant.

Her ears felt the pain so did her body. She became terribly dizzy and weak.

She saw an episode of lords Shiv's serial and slept so that she could die in peace that it would really be a miracle if she lived.

That night with tears in her eyes, she kissed the shivling on her rudraksha amulet. Her tears fell on the shivling on the little emulet.

Lord Shiv was touched by her devotion, and so was lord Krishna. They both destroyed the poison in her body, due to her piety.

Next morning Swati woke up with a dizzy head.

She saw the rudraksha amulet had melodramatically broken into two pieces. (It was symbolic of lord breaking up with her for such stupid act like suicide).She was surprised at her life.

"I ate sleeping pills" she confessed to her grandmother.

What! She exclaimed in anger.

What followed was a morning fiasco that day, with everybody screaming at her for her pitiable act. When her grandmother calmed down next day, She asked how many pills did you eat that day?

26 grandma.. she replied with a sad face.

What 26 ! She exclaimed. "I can't bear even 10, surely a miracle saved you my child."

"Yes Ma".. She smiled and thanked Lord Shiv and Lord Krishna for saving her life.

She realised she would have died that day but lord took her poison. The Shivling had absorbed the poison that's why it broke into two pieces.

God broke up with his devotee in compassion that day to give Swati a new life.

After a few days, She met a really nice guy on facebook by the grace of Shiv. His name was Bhaskar. He was really handsome and intelligent. An engineer. He was really sympathetic to her condition. A new boyfriend just like she wanted. Her condition gradually improved, and she got intertwined with her normal life again.

As they say life and love never ends.

All the kind and heartbroken Lord Shiv said was **"wait for me beloved, in the myriad sands of time. No more not yet.."**

"I'll live with you even if not yours so that you smile still when on Kailash you meditate, fighting my monsters with god by my side, for you soul still lives in me.. as a spark that gives me hope that one day you may unite." Swati.. She is still his devotee but now lives a healthy and normal life.

<u>Poem</u>

I shivered as a butterfly
when you came to me as a monster
who protected me as my beloved
from the rest who snapped
my loving lord, how time changes men
but still its not you' re fault
just waves of destiny
Be my flower next life
then I'll be you're butterfly again
this curse of time against mounds of my sand
in infinity of thine presence
how I submissed in the ocean of thine strong arms
like a wife's pious submission
to her beloved lord
What they know, how safe I feel
In your innocence and guile
that I still want to work to make you smile
to inspire you love
An ocean of ego is rare to cross
A mountain of ego is rare to descend
That they may scorn,
then they'll be forlorn

for what I had they can only dream..
your beating heart in my heart
for they can only dream.. for they can only dream..

CHAPTER FIVE

TO LAUKESH WITH LOVE..

In the mountains of Kailash.. stood a pious devotee meditating on his lord. His name was Laukesh. He was a very naïve man and an ardent devotee of Lord Shiv. He meditated for 50 years and gained the respect of lord Shiv.

He was revered by Gods and kings alike.

One day when he was meditating suddenly Lord Indra appeared.

How are you my humble man.. he asked. He scattered his ruffled hairs that ended in curls and bowed to the lord. "In this desolated place, no one comes as this is my secret place for penace. Who are you gentleman?" he asked slowly. He must be Lord Indra or one of his sons he thought.

"I am the Lord Indra." After exchanging pleasantries Lord said to him "It's been 50 years of your life Laukesh.. Shiv won't come. Why don't you go back to you're village and marry some good girl.

This angered the saint as he had left all worldly relations behind.

Lord Indra laughed and said "No dear I am your devotee. You will be the supreme king in the future that is why I want you to stop you're penace and enjoy worldly pleasures."

"What supreme king ? I have no interest in titles or worldly desires." He said.

Thus Lord laughed in chivalry and said that it's lesser than Shiv.

Laukesh made a frowny face and said "I don't want to be anything lesser than Shiv".

"Okay my dear devotee..I will always be your friend if you want but please stop you're penace".

Laukesh refused and pushed him away. "I will curse you if you distract me again" shouted Lokesh

The arrogant Indra went away in haste.

He continued penace for 10 years more.

So after 55 years of penace Lord Shiv appeared and gave him blessings.

So Lord Shiv appeared only to test his devotion. He knew Lord Shiv as a celibate unmarried demigod from his time.

Lord Shiv appeared with a shivling in his hand.

"Om Namah Shivay" He commanded.

Laukesh opened his eyes and smiled. Oh my lord its you. He fell on his feet and immediately pulled a big stone for him to sit.

How are you my dearest son. I am pleased by you're devotion. What shall I give you. Any materialistic or spiritual power not attainable by you I can give you as a blessing.

He asked nothing but said that please let me enter Kailash with you. I want to meet you're family.

Shiv lovingly smiled and said O' my beloved Laukesh Is that all you need, then I will take you but remember that this world is my family.I have everyone and yet no one in attachment.

To which laukesh started crying..Lord Shiv has no one then my Lord should marry me to have a wife and family.

Lord Shiv laughed heartily. Had you been a woman I wouldn't have said no but in the present I am married so let me take you to my wife Parvati. The great demigod of time bent before the Lord and asked "where should I take the two gentlemen".

"My Dear time take my beloved Laukesh to the time where I am married to Parvati".

"So be it" said the demigod of time.

Lord Shiv could travel to future but to go in past needed a lot of penace.

They appeared on Kailash. Parvati welcomed them with open arms.

"Is this you're sister Shiv" he asked.

Shiv smiled hell no..This is my loving wife and there are my two kids. The two kids ran and hugged him calling him uncle! uncle!

He was confused. He said my lord you are not my Shiv ,My Lord was a celibate.My heart is not able to accept you as a married man. I remained alone only to please you my lord.

Saying thus heartbroken Laukesh engrossed himself in penace again.

Shiv ji understood his pain. Thus he too disappeared in a secret cave ,and meditated for a thousand year. "My devotee shall not suffer due to my marriage" he said to himself. His hairs grew long with time and bones emerged yet he kept meditating.

Lord Vishnu appeared. "I am pleased with your devotion, my brother Shiv, what is it that you desire?" he asked.

"I need your powers to go into the past, for my dear devotee Laukesh is not able to accept me as a married man. I need to take him into the past to my celibate form" replied Shiv.

"So be it" and saying thus Lord Vishnu granted his wish.

He called upon secret meditative powers from Vishnu the supreme lord.Thus Lord Shiv took Laukesh into the past where the lord was a celibate. Seeing his lord in a celibate form,tears grew in the eyes of his devotee and he fell unto his feet. Thus Lord Shiv went back in time to his celibate form so that Laukesh does not get a shock. This story has a beautiful ending. Later the mendicant merged into the holy form of Lord Shiv by tapasya and got salvation in the divine.

My darling Lord.. you are the zenith of my sea
Just be in my breath
and I can see
my kind king
feeling you from a distance
for you are the breath of Sea..
Menace menace every where
breathe away my strife
We shall meet again in time, my shy lord in penace
O' The greatest of the sages
Controller of the time
there is nothing I need in life
This whole world just moves on and on
Its time which thus dictates
So trapped I felt in this material world
Like a fish in a bait
Yet my lord is so kind and humble
A thousand years no food or sleep
He loves his humble devotee thus

AN ODYSSEY

For me he became a celibate
For me he became a celibate..

CHAPTER SIX

WHEN THE LORD READ FOR HIS DEVOTEE

Once upon a time in the state of Kerala, in a temple called Kottiyoor, the main deity was Lord Shiva. In the same place lived an ardent devotee of Krishna named Poonthaanam. His devotion transcended the boundaries of heart and soul. The temple opened only during winters and was closed for the rest of the year, sans any human activities. One day, after taking bath in the holy river, Poonthaanam was elated and was singing hymns for Lord Shiva. He recited the Bhagwat Katha in front of Lord Shiva's idol every day. Hundreds of people gathered to listen to his discourse on the divine tales of Lord Krishna and his beautiful queen Rukmini. One day, Poonthaanam recited the story from the tenth canto of Srimad Bhagavatam; it was named "Lord Krishna plays with Queen Rukmini."

In this story, the lord was playing with his beloved wife Rukmini and started teasing her. He playfully asked her why she had married him, especially when she had had other options, like her ex-fiancé Shishupal. He further teased her by saying that she should consider a divorce as he had become bored of a married life and wanted to live like an ascetic. Listening to such harsh words, Rukmini fainted, as if her whole world had collapsed. Later, the lord consoled her and apologised.

After Poonthaanam finished the discourse, he left a bookmark at the last page of the story. Next day, to his amazement, the bookmark had moved to the start of the same chapter. So the priest read the same story again. This routine went on for many days until the last day of closure of the temple. As the temple was closing for the year, Poonthaanam walked out of the temple. Suddenly he remembered that he had left the holy Bhagavatam in the temple itself.

He walked rapidly towards the temple, and when he reached there, he was all alone. Suddenly, he heard a voice reading from the same chapter in the Bhagavatam; the voice came from inside the temple premises. But the gate was locked. He looked through the keyhole of the door. Whom did he see but Lord Shiva, sitting beside a tree and reading Poonthaanam's Bhagavatam?

The kind mother Parvati and other ghosts were also present. They were listening to the lord, overwhelmed with tears of devotion.

Poonthaanam was motionless as he heard the whole discourse.

At the end of the recitation, Lord Shiva asked his wife Parvati, "Did you like the recitation?"

"Yes, it was nice," Parvathi replied, "but not as good as Poonthaanam's."

The sweet lord replied, "Yes, that is true. I also like to hear Bhagavatam from Poonthaanam. That is why I placed the bookmark again and again at the beginning of the same chapter every day."

On hearing this, Poonthaanam was shaken up and loudly uttered the holy name of Krishna.

When he peeked through the keyhole again, Lord Shiva and Mother Parvathi had disappeared.

Moral of the story:

This story clearly explains how all the living entities, including the demigods, love this great literature.

Srimad Bhagavatam (verse 12.13.18) says:

srimad bhagavatam puranam amalam yad vaishnavaanaam priyam

yasmin paaramahamsyam ekam amalam jnaanam param geeyate

tatra jnaana viraaga bhakti sahitam naishkarmyam aavishkrtam

tac chrnvan supathan vicaarana paro bhaktyaa vimucyen narah

"Srimad Bhagavatam is the spotless purana. It is most dear to the Vaishnavas because it describes the pure and supreme knowledge of the paramahamsas (honorific for Hindu spiritual leaders who have become enlightened). This Bhagavatam reveals the means for becoming free from all material possessions, together with the processes of transcendental knowledge, renunciation and devotion. Anyone who seriously tries to understand the Srimad Bhagavatam, who properly hears and chants it with devotion, becomes completely liberated."

The word paaramahamsyam indicates that even completely liberated souls are eager to hear and narrate the Srimad Bhagavatam.

Hare Krishna, Hare Krishna, Krishna Krishna, Hare Hare

Hare Rama, Hare Rama, Rama Rama, Hare Hare.